The Mystery
of the Czar

Penn Mullin

High Noon Books
Novato, California

Cover Design and Interior Illustrations: Nancy Peach

International Standard Book Number: 1-57128-058-8

9 8 7 6 5 4 3 2 1 0
2 1 0 9 8 7 6 5 4 3

Contents

Corina and Zack are young co-workers at the Park Museum. They are assistants to the museum's director, Claire Long, who sends them to the "four corners of the world" on exciting explorations.

CHAPTER 1

Come to St. Petersburg!

"Look at this! I just got an e-mail from my friend Vanya (VON-ya) in Russia," Corina told Zack. "She's in charge of a big show at the Hermitage museum in St. Petersburg."

"I remember Vanya!" Zack said. He looked over Corina's shoulder at her laptop computer screen and read: "'I'm up to my ears with this Fabergé (fah-ber-JHEY) show! So much work. Would the Park Museum let you come over to help me set up the show?'"

"I want to do it!" said Corina. "We could both go. Wouldn't that be super?"

"Sure! But how do we get our museum to agree to this plan?" laughed Zack.

"Claire has always wanted to have a show of Fabergé's work here. She loves the jewelry he designed and his Easter eggs with the surprises inside." Corina smiled. "What if . . . ?"

"Ah ha! I see a plan here," Zack chuckled.

"Maybe we could work a deal with Vanya. We go help her now, and then she helps us bring the Fabergé show over here!" said Corina. "Let's go see Claire and ask her!"

Corina jumped up from her desk and pulled Zack out the door towards Claire's office.

CHAPTER 2

A Mystery to Solve

"Wow! We're in Russia and I'm not freezing!" said Zack. "The sun is even shining!"

"This is July!" laughed Corina. "Vanya knew she'd never get me here in the winter!"

"It's great we can stay with her," said Zack. "I guess she'll take us to her apartment from the museum. I'm feeling pretty wiped out from that plane trip! How many hours?"

"Too many!" Corina yawned. "It was wild trying to get here so fast. But these 2 weeks are the only ones Claire said we could have."

"Sounds like Vanya *can* help us get the Fabergé show to our museum. Claire was ready to deal when she heard that," Zack said. "And I want to know more about that last e-mail message when Vanya said: 'Corina, you always love mysteries. And I've got one waiting for you!'" Zack smiled. "What do you think it is?"

"I don't know. Vanya and I had a great time when we were in college solving mysteries like who was stealing ice cream from the dorm freezer." Corina laughed. "We never did anything big."

Suddenly a taxi pulled up and they climbed in with their bags.

"The Hermitage museum please," Zack said.

"Welcome to St. Petersburg! My name is Alexi (a-LEX-ee). Is this your first time here?" the taxi driver asked.

"Yes," said Corina. "We're Corina and Zack, Alexi. Are you from St. Petersburg?"

"Yes, this is my city. Wait till you see the beautiful Old City! Right now all you see is this." He pointed to the miles of tall apartment buildings on both sides of the freeway. "Only Moscow is bigger than us now."

"You speak English well," Zack said.

"Thank you. I was a guide for Americans and English people around this city," Alexi said.

"That was when it was called Leningrad, for the Russian leader Lenin. I was glad they gave it back its old name a few years ago – St. Petersburg. Because it *is* the city of Peter the Great. He was the Czar (ZAR) who built it as the capital in the early 1700's."

"The capital was moved to Moscow after the 1917 revolution, wasn't it?" Zack asked.

"Yes. Russia was changed forever. The Czars no longer ruled. The Soviet Union was set up as a government instead. This was to give more power to the people," Alexi said.

"But that didn't work – the Soviet Union no longer exists today. Russia has really had a lot of changes, hasn't it?" said Corina.

"Yes, and things are getting better with our new government now." Alexi pointed out the window. "Look – we are in the Old City!"

"This looks like Paris – not Russia!" Zack said. "The big wide open squares and beautiful old buildings."

"That's what Peter the Great wanted," said Alexi. "This was to be Russia's show-off city to the rest of Europe. This street Nevsky Prospect leads right to the Winter Palace."

"We were so lucky to get you for our taxi driver, Alexi!" Corina said.

"I love to show off my city." Alexi smiled. He soon turned into a huge beautiful open space by the river.

"Palace Square." Alexi told them. "So much history happened here. Most of the revolutions began right here in front of the Czar's home: The Winter Palace." He pointed to the huge building that stretched all the way to the river bank.

"That is amazing!" Zack whistled.

"Only about 1,000 rooms," laughed Alexi. "Shall I take you to the main entrance?"

"Yes, thanks, Alexi. Our friend is waiting for us in there – somewhere! Will we ever find her office, Zack?"

"I'll leave that to you, Corina," laughed Zack. "You're the one who's good at mysteries!"

CHAPTER 3

Vanya's Museum

"Corina! You're here!" A small blond-haired woman ran towards them down the hall. She and Corina grabbed each other in a hug.

"Gosh, it's been so long, Vanya! You're looking great," Corina said.

"I work too hard now! After this show, I'm taking a vacation. Zack, hey!" Vanya gave him a hug, too. "It's great to see you. You two are super to come over here to help me out."

"Well, you're helping us, too," Corina said.

"Claire is really excited about our museum's getting the Fabergé show."

"And I may just have to come over to help set it up," Vanya said. "In the middle of winter when I never see the sun over here! Come, let's put your bags in my office."

Soon they entered a large pale blue and gold room with white carpeting. In one corner of it was a huge table piled high with papers.

"What a beautiful office!" Corina whispered. "But the same old Vanya desk!" she laughed. "Just like back in college."

"You can never impress old friends," Vanya chuckled. "Gosh, it's great to see you two. Corina, you're too skinny. Just like always. Got to fatten you up with some Russian *blini*! Remember those little pancakes my mother used to make for us and fill with jam?"

"Oh, yes!" Corina rolled her eyes. "So, Vanya, how can we help you with your show?"

"Well, so much of Fabergé's work has come in for the show: his jewelry, clocks, his famous Easter eggs," Vanya explained. "Museums and owners worldwide have lent pieces."

"So we can help with all the paperwork, keep track of what comes in," Zack said.

"Just put us to work. We're a good team, Zack and I," Corina laughed.

"Wonderful! Well, come with me. I want to

show you some of our treasures here. Then we'll go to my place. You must be wiped out by now!" Vanya led them down a wide hallway whose walls were lined with mirrors and gold.

"This part of the Winter Palace was once a retreat, a place to be alone. That's how it got the name of 'Hermitage.' Here the Czars began putting all the art they collected," Vanya said. "And now this museum has one of the richest art collections in the world."

She stopped in front of a large doorway with guards on either side. They nodded at her, and Vanya led Corina and Zack inside a room that dazzled their eyes. Gold and silver objects glittered from shelves all around them. "This is

12

*Vanya led them down a wide hallway whose walls
were lined with mirrors and gold.*

the Special Collection," she said. "So many of Fabergé's finest pieces." She pointed to shelves full of tiny jeweled pillboxes and brightly-colored animals. Then she stopped at a large table with a glass top. Corina and Zack looked inside and gasped.

"The Fabergé Easter eggs! Look, Zack, the Coronation Egg," Corina whispered.

They stared down at the golden egg lying on the white cloth. It was about 5 inches high. Gold bands of leaves, tiny eagles, and diamonds crisscrossed all over it.

Vanya was unlocking the case. "This was given to the Czarina (zar-EE-na) Alexandra by her husband Czar Nicholas II on Easter in 1897 just after their coronation. Easter was the most important holiday of the year in Russia. Each year the Czar would ask the jeweler Carl Fabergé to create special eggs for his wife and mother. Each egg took a year to make." Vanya carefully picked up the egg.

"It is so perfect," whispered Corina.

Vanya touched a certain spot on the egg, and the top part of the egg swung upward!

"Amazing!" said Zack. Inside was a tiny golden coach, complete in every detail.

"It's the coronation coach," Vanya explained. She carefully lifted it out of the egg and set it in Corina's hand. "Look at the tiny wheels and the glass window. Exactly like the real coach for the coronation."

"Look – the wheels go around and the little steps even fold down!" said Zack.

"What is this little hook inside the carriage?" Corina asked. "Was something on it?"

"Yes – a tiny diamond egg. It disappeared long ago. Thank heavens not since it was here at the museum! So many of the treasures inside the eggs have mysteriously disappeared over the years," Vanya said.

"Speaking of mysteries, what were you talking about in that e-mail?" Corina asked.

Vanya looked over her shoulder and lowered her voice. "I'll tell you about it later when we're alone. Now is not the time."

CHAPTER 4

A Message of Danger

Vanya drove slowly through the crowded streets of St. Petersburg's rush hour.

"I'm still in a daze from seeing those amazing Fabergé eggs," Corina told her friend.

"My favorite was the railroad egg!" said Zack. "I couldn't believe that tiny perfect train inside the egg. And it actually ran!"

"How many eggs did Fabergé design?" Corina asked.

"54 – that we know of," Vanya said. "But

there may be one more! And this is the mystery I want to tell you about! You know that the Russian people rebelled against the Czar in 1917. The country had been weakened by World War I. People were starving. They felt that the Czar was a poor ruler, not paying attention to their needs. The Czar, his wife, and their 5 children were imprisoned."

"Where were they in prison?" Zack asked.

"At a place in the country a few hours' drive from here," Vanya said.

"Is that where they all were killed?"

"Yes, the revolutionaries shot them in November of 1918," Vanya said. "It shocked the world. A terrible tragedy. And this is where the mystery comes in."

"This sounds spooky," said Corina.

"I have a good friend Leon (LEE-on) who works with me. He has found out that there *was* one more egg made for the Czar in 1917. But it was kept secret so the revolutionaries would not get it. We think the Czar carried it secretly out of the palace and hid it in the house where he was held prisoner."

"Fantastic!" Zack said.

"I would love to find that missing egg!" Vanya smiled. "And present it to the world at our big museum show. But we may be too late. Someone may have found it long ago. Or maybe the Czar never got it out of the palace. Do you want to help me look for it?"

"Yes!" Corina and Zack both said at once.

"Good! There's one thing, though. It might be dangerous. The wrong kind of people may also be looking for the egg. To sell on the black market. Anyway, here's my plan," Vanya told them. "We'll leave early tomorrow for Ekaterinburg (e-CAT-er-in-burg), where the Czar and his family were imprisoned. I'm borrowing a car so we won't be followed – hopefully. My friend Leon will meet us later."

"Does anyone live there now – at the place where they were held?" Corina asked.

"Yes, a wonderful old couple. They have owned it for fifty years. This is all a big surprise to them about the egg. They want to help us all they can," Vanya said.

"This is really exciting, Vanya! You're going to let us in on it all!" said Zack.

"Well, here is where I live." Vanya turned into a large garage under her building. Then they took the elevator up to her apartment. "Welcome," she said as opened the door.

Both Corina and Zack were surprised at how small Vanya's place was.

"This is big compared to my last place!" Vanya laughed. "There are long waiting lists for larger apartments."

"But you made it cozy and you have a great view all over the city," said Corina.

Vanya went over to the computer on her desk and turned it on. "There's a message from Leon here. He's using our secret code. Uh-oh, he was followed today on his way to Ekaterinburg. So he stopped early. He's staying in a nearby town. The guys who followed him are looking for him. He says for us to go to the house on a different road and he'll keep the guys busy in town. You two still want to do this?"

"Of course!" said Zack. "More than ever!"

"I don't have a cellular phone yet. Hard to get them over here," Vanya said. "So let's bring your laptop. Then we can send out for help – just in case!"

CHAPTER 5

"Keep the Laptop Close By!"

It was barely dawn when they set out in a borrowed car on the road to Ekaterinburg.

"I'm sure not awake yet!" Zack yawned. "It never got dark last night. I couldn't fall asleep in broad daylight."

"That's July in Russia," Vanya laughed. "There's still daylight at 11. But in winter, the sun forgets us! It gets dark so early."

Soon they were driving through beautiful green farmlands. They could see people already at work in the wheatfields.

"Help me watch for someone following us," Vanya said. "I sure hope Leon is O.K. He didn't tell me the name of the town he's in. He knows I'd go there to find him instead of going to look for the egg."

"I wonder how these other people found out about the egg," said Corina.

"There's always a leak. Somebody sells information. You try to be careful, but people always find out," Vanya sighed.

"Have you searched the house at all yet for the egg?" Zack asked.

"Just a little. There are some barns there, too, that we need to check," Vanya said.

They drove on through the countryside for another hour. No one following so far!

"We're getting close now," Vanya said. Soon they drove through a wooden gate and up a long road. A large stone house looked rather like a gloomy fortress. "This is it. It's easy to believe the terrible things that happened here."

A smiling gray-haired elderly couple came out of the front door to welcome them.

"Olga! Carl! It's good to see you again," said Vanya as she got out of the car. "These are my American friends Corina and Zack."

"Welcome to our home," Olga told Corina and Zack. "You have come a very long way. We hope you will find what you are looking for."

A large stone house looked rather like a gloomy fortress.

"Thank you," Corina and Zack told them.

"Has there been any message from Leon?" Vanya asked Olga and Carl.

"None. Is he coming, too?" Carl asked.

"We hope so," Vanya said. "Have any strangers come since I was last here?"

"None," said Olga. "At least we have not *seen* anyone. Do others know about the secret?"

"I'm afraid so," Vanya said. "The wrong kind of people. I don't want you to be in any danger. If you do not want us to search here, that is fine. This is your home."

"Oh, no! We want you to stay and search. The egg belongs to Russia. We are not afraid," Olga said. "I will keep watch down the road."

"You are wonderful," Vanya told them. "First I need to call the police in the nearest village and get their e-mail number. Also, I'm going to ask them to check for messages every few minutes. Just in case we need to reach them quickly."

"But we have a phone," Carl said.

"Phone lines are easily cut," Vanya told him. "We could be trapped out here with no way to call for help. Our computer has no wires."

They all went inside the house, and Vanya checked in with the police.

"Now I feel better," she said. "I got their number. I wish I knew if that is the village where Leon is right now. He is being followed,

28

Olga and Carl. He is trying to keep the men away from here while we search."

"I hope you find the egg soon, and take it to safety at the Hermitage," Olga said.

"Let's begin!" Vanya said. "Carl, will you show Zack the Czar's bedroom and sitting room? You two could do another check in there. Closets, loose floorboards, cupboards. Corina, you and I will search the Czarina's rooms. Olga, thank you for being our lookout."

"I will watch very carefully!" the old woman said. "Do not worry."

"Corina, don't forget to bring along your laptop," Vanya said. "Let's keep it close by."

They all split up to go to different parts of

the large old house.

They came to the bedroom of the Czarina. All the furniture was of dark, heavy wood. The curtains, rugs, and bedspread were all a deep velvety blue. Corina felt a shiver go down her spine as she entered the room.

"It's sad to think of that family as prisoners here. Those children," Corina said.

"I know. I really feel their presence in these rooms, too," Vanya said.

"I'll start looking in the closet first. I see there are a lot of built-in drawers there." Corina went into the large dark room.

"Check for drawers with false backs," Vanya said. "People used to hide things in those. I'll check the floor boards in this other closet to see if any are loose."

"The egg belonged to the Czarina. So it makes sense that she might be the one to hide it," Corina said. She pulled open the old wooden drawers and put her hand into each one. "It's a weird feeling to think that the Czarina herself once had her hand in these!"

Corina checked all the drawers and then the floorboards of the closet. But everything was empty, nothing was loose. She next started checking floorboards in the bedroom.

"It could take us several days to get through the whole house and barns," Vanya said. "And I'm worried about Leon. Later on we can drive around through the nearby towns and see if we can spot his car parked somewhere."

"Maybe the guys following him lost interest and went on. That's what I hope," Corina said. "But he might be afraid to come here yet in case they were still following."

"You're right. We may just have to wait."

Soon Carl called up the stairs, "Come down and have some coffee Olga has made!"

"We'll be right down!" Vanya called.

"I'll just wash up and come down," Corina said, going into the Czarina's bathroom.

"See you downstairs," said Vanya.

Corina turned on the water in the old sink and washed her face and hands. Suddenly she dropped her ring onto the bathroom floor. It rolled behind the sink. She had to get down on her hands and knees to reach it. And then she saw something else! A small square piece of the back of the sink had fallen away – and there was a perfectly cut hole! Corina's heart began to pound. Could it be? Should she stick her hand inside? She slowly slipped her hand down into the hole. What would she feel? Nothing but air? Spiders? Then she felt something hard and smooth. Her fingers closed around it and she pulled it out of the hole. It was a purple box! Her hands shook as she pressed the tiny clasp and opened it. There on a bed of white cloth lay a perfect lilac-colored egg covered by tiny flowers of pearls and diamonds! She tried to open her mouth to call Vanya and Zack, but no sound came out. All she could do was stare at this treasure.

Finally she stood up shakily and started downstairs with the egg in her hand. Suddenly she heard loud voices below.

"So – you thought you were the only ones who knew about the egg, didn't you, Vanya? Well, you were wrong. We found your friend's car. And this map. We figured out where you were," an ugly voice snarled.

Corina tiptoed back into the bedroom. No one had seen her in the hall. The laptop! Get the laptop. Type in the number and the SOS code

Vanya had taped to it. Smart Vanya. Thank you.
Corina's hand shook as she turned on the
computer and typed in a message to the police
to come quickly. Please, don't let the men come
up here, she prayed. The egg. I've got to hide it.
She tiptoed into the bathroom and put the egg
back into the hole behind the sink. What to do
now? She could still hear the voices downstairs.
Zack and Vanya were probably trying to keep
the men talking, stalling them so she would
have time to call the police before they came
upstairs. She should get away from this room so
close to the egg. But how? Suddenly she heard
the men start up the stairs!

CHAPTER 6

Prisoners!

She met them in the hall. There were two of them, and they were huge and cruel looking.

"So – one more of you. Hiding up here? Or were you up here looking for something?" The large man was out of breath after the stairs. He had a long ugly scar across his cheek.

"I'm sick. I was lying down in there." Corina pointed to another bedroom.

"I bet. You're in on this search, too. Well, you and your pals are going to take a little walk," the scarred man told Corina. He turned to his partner. "You look around up here. There might be more of them. Good thing we cut the phone line."

Please let the police get that message, please! thought Corina as she went down the stairs. Where were the others? What did the man mean: take a little walk? She felt sick with fear. She saw the gun at the man's waist.

The man led her out into the kitchen. There she saw Olga, Carl, Vanya and Zack huddled together in a corner. Another man stood with them with a rifle across his chest.

"Corina!" Zack reached out and pulled her into their group. She couldn't stop shaking.

"O.K., Brown's going to take you guys on a walk. Don't give him any trouble. Just do what he says." The scarred man turned to go.

Please don't let him find the egg, please! Corina thought. She stumbled along with the others out into the backyard of the house. They were headed towards a large barn. Brown walked behind them with his rifle. We shouldn't go into that barn. We can't! Maybe they should rush the guard! If she could just talk to Zack or Vanya. Tell them she'd called the police. But no one said a word. No one trusted the man with the rifle behind them.

Carl got to the barn first and slid the door open. They went inside into the darkness one by one. Corina reached for Zack's hand.

"Sit down," Brown ordered. They all sat down together in a pile of hay on the floor. Brown stood over them with his rifle. His face was set in a grim smile. What was being planned for them by these awful men? Suddenly Corina thought of the Czar, his wife, their children. Was it in here, perhaps that –

Suddenly they heard cars skidding to a stop on the gravel outside! Loud voices. What was happening? Brown looked worried. He began backing towards the barn door. Then suddenly the door swung open! Light streamed inside. Men rushed in. "Police! Freeze!" someone yelled. Brown threw down his rifle.

CHAPTER 7

Corina's Secret

Everyone was crowded around Corina out in front of the old house.

"You're amazing!" Zack told Corina. "If you hadn't used the laptop to call . . ."

Corina stopped him. "Thank Vanya. She told us to bring the laptop with us."

"We were lucky. Really lucky," Vanya said. "That one with the scar is one of the worst in Russia. Leon, I'm so glad you're safe, too!" She grinned at the tall man beside her whose head was in a bandage. Those men really tried hard to make sure you wouldn't call the police after they stole your car."

"When I woke up and got to the police station, your message had just come through on the Internet, Corina," Leon said.

Corina had been saving her secret until now. "Everybody, I've got something to show you." She smiled mysteriously. "Follow me." She led the group quickly up the stairs and into the Czarina's bedroom.

"Corina, is it the egg? Did you find the egg?" Vanya cried. "Tell us!"

Corina just smiled and stepped into the bathroom. She bent down and reached behind the bottom of the sink. Then her hand felt the smooth box and she slowly lifted it out.

"Ohhhhhhh!" everyone said at once. She slowly opened the lid to show the beautiful egg inside. Then she put it in Vanya's hand.

"It is perfect," whispered Vanya. "The final egg the Czar ever gave his wife. Her favorite color – lavendar. These lilies of the valley were the flower she liked best."

"Is there a secret button?" Zack asked.

Leon gently pressed one of the pearls. The top of the egg swung upward to show a tiny silver dog inside.

"It's her favorite pet, her dachshund (DOXZ-hund)!" said Vanya. "What a wonderful

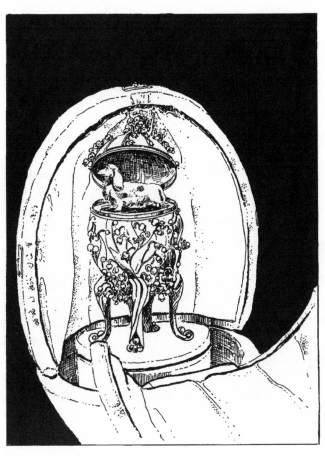

Leon gently pressed one of the pearls.
The top of the egg swung upward to show
a tiny silver dog inside.

thoughtful gift."

"Corina, how did you ever find this behind the *sink*?" asked Zack.

"I dropped my ring. It went behind there and that's how I saw the secret hole."

"Lucky ring, too! Thanks for bringing that luck to Russia, my dear! Say, do you think your boss would let you stay here maybe six months longer?" Vanya laughed. "You could stand by this special new egg at the Hermitage show and tell the story of how it was found."

"I think I'll wait and do that when the egg comes to our museum," Corina laughed. "We need to keep Claire happy so we can go on more trips! Right, Zack?"